Illustrations on pages 28-29: © Larousse, C. Beaumont,
F. Bouttevin, P. Morin, O. Nadel
Animal facts: Miguel Larzillière

First edition
2 4 6 8 10 9 7 5 3 1

Library of Congress Cataloging-in-Publication Data
Doinet, Mymi.
Dolphin/ story by Mymi Doinet ;
illustrations by Clara Nomdedeu and Christophe Merlin.
p. cm. – (Abbeville Animals)
Summary: When he finds his friend Odene caught in coral and being
threatened by a white shark, Little Blue, a young Dolphin, enlists the
help of the other dolphins, a blue whale, and a school of parrot-fish
to rescue her.
ISBN 0-7892-0661-7 (alk. paper)
Dolphins—Juvenile fiction.
[1. Dolphins—Fiction. 2.Animals—Infancy—Fiction.]
I. Nomdedeu, Clara, ill. II. Merlin, C. (Christophe), ill. III. Title. IV. Series.

PZ10.3.D7108 Do 2000
[E]—dc21   00-022080

Abbeville Animals

Dolphin

By Mymi Doinet
Illustrations by Clara Nomdedeu and Christophe Merlin
Translation by Roger Pasquier

Abbeville Kids
A Division of Abbeville Publishing Group
New York • London • Paris

In the deep blue ocean, Little Blue moves slowly through the seaweed. He gulps down dozens of little shrimp. Rocked by the waves, he soon closes one eye, then the other. Little Blue falls asleep. . . .

Little Blue dreams that he is leaping over the clouds. He says to himself, "Tonight, I'll catch some shooting stars, and make them float in the sea like little boats." Then Little Blue wakes up with a start. Someone is sobbing among the waves.

8

The dolphin lives in water, but is not a fish. It breathes air through a blowhole, a small opening on the top of its head.

Dolphins can jump over twenty feet in the air—higher than a two-story building!

Little Blue discovers a huge, steaming volcano. Behind the fumes he finds Ondene, a young dolphin trapped in some coral. She cries out, "Help me! I'm stuck, and there are sharks nearby!"

For orcas and white sharks, tuna and salmon are only a mouthful. Sometimes they also attack dolphins.

Beneath the sea, dolphins may see mountains of red coral, and then swim above what are really volcanoes spewing out boiling water.

Little Blue whistles, "Quick, we have to save Ondene."

His cousins hurry to help. Suddenly, an enormous wave sends them tumbling. Little Blue trembles with fear, thinking some sharks are coming.

When alarmed, a dolphin whistles, and the other dolphins gather. In a group, they are stronger when facing any danger.

...Bla bla bla....

Dolphins recognize each other by their chatter. The clapping of their beaks sounds like the creaking of a door.

13

It's Bella, the giant blue whale. She
sings a strange little song:
"I know how we can save Ondene.
So come, let's see what will be seen!"
Swimming with Bella, the dolphins
pass through a school of sardines. But
where is Bella taking them?

Dolphins eat sardines, crabs,
squid, and shrimp. They swallow
them whole, eating about
twenty-five pounds a day.

Adult dolphins have many
small, pointed teeth.

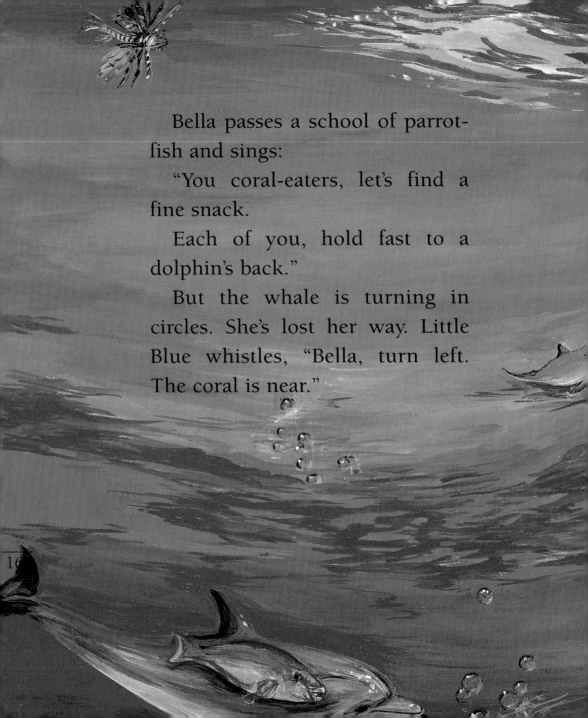

Bella passes a school of parrot-fish and sings:

"You coral-eaters, let's find a fine snack.

Each of you, hold fast to a dolphin's back."

But the whale is turning in circles. She's lost her way. Little Blue whistles, "Bella, turn left. The coral is near."

The dolphin's forehead sends out high-pitched sounds. Like an echo, these sounds bounce back from anything around the dolphin. The dolphin then knows its distance to other objects, from sharks to sardines.

Dolphins help each other. When one of them is sick, the others bring it to the surface of the water so it can breathe.

The hungry parrot-fish chew away at the coral, and it falls apart. Ondene calls out, "Thank you, friends. Thank you, Little Blue." Suddenly, from far away, a noise like thunder echoes. Little Blue and his friends scatter.

20

Courting dolphins dance together, leaping over the waves.

It's a shark, arriving too late to attack the trapped dolphin. The dolphins are already far away. Safe from the shark, they celebrate the rescue of Ondene. She and Little Blue open the dance, and all their friends twirl with them under the blue waves.

Dolphins caress each other with little strokes of their fins, and then nip at each other as a kind of kiss.

All About Dolphins

A dolphin is a kind of whale. Dolphins live in warm and temperate waters.

The young dolphin develops for a year in the belly of its mother, protected by a sack of fluid. When it is born, the dolphin already knows how to swim.

When giving birth, a mother dolphin is helped by one or two older females. They push the newborn to the surface so it can take its first breath of air.

The dolphin is a mammal, like the cat, the horse, and the elephant. Young dolphins suck thick and nourishing milk from the breast of the mother dolphin.

Dolphins must come to the surface every few minutes to breathe. Like humans, they could die from lack of air.

Dolphins live in groups. Females and their young swim in the center. At the front and the rear, the males protect them.

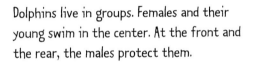

Dolphins are not afraid of people. They often come close to boats, and swim in the waves following the bow. Sometimes, they also approach swimmers.

In Africa, dolphins help fishermen. They drive fish toward the nets. Dolphins help themselves, too, when they catch some of the fish that jump out of the water.

An adult dolphin may grow to be ten feet long, the length of a small boat.

Its blowhole is round, like a little nostril. When the blowhole is closed, the dolphin can stay underwater for several minutes.

On its forehead the dolphin has a big bump. This is called the melon; it makes high-pitched sounds.

The dolphin has a beak made of two long jaws that seem to be smiling.

It has many small, sharp teeth.

Its eyes see equally well in and out of the water.

It weighs more than 550 pounds, equal to a dozen six-year-old children.

The dolphin uses its dorsal fin to keep its balance.

By moving its tail fin up and down, the dolphin can glide through the water at thirty miles per hour.

The dolphin steers to the left or right with its pectoral fins.

Its skin is soft. Drops of water slide off it like water slides off a raincoat.

Follow the Path

Have fun following the dolphin's path and answering the questions

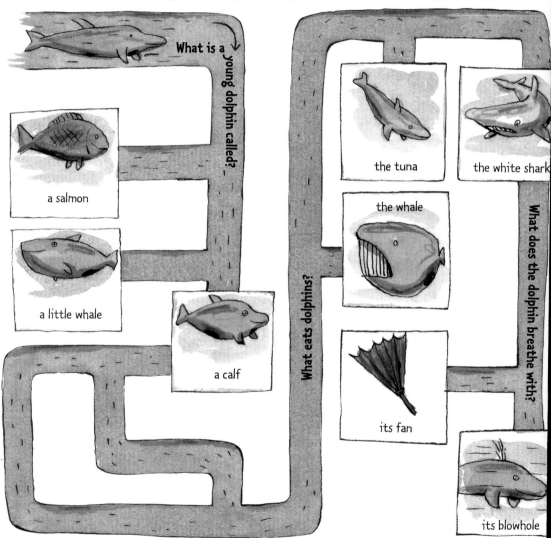

What is a young dolphin called?

a salmon

a little whale

a calf

What eats dolphins?

the tuna

the white shark

the whale

its fan

What does the dolphin breathe with?

its blowhole

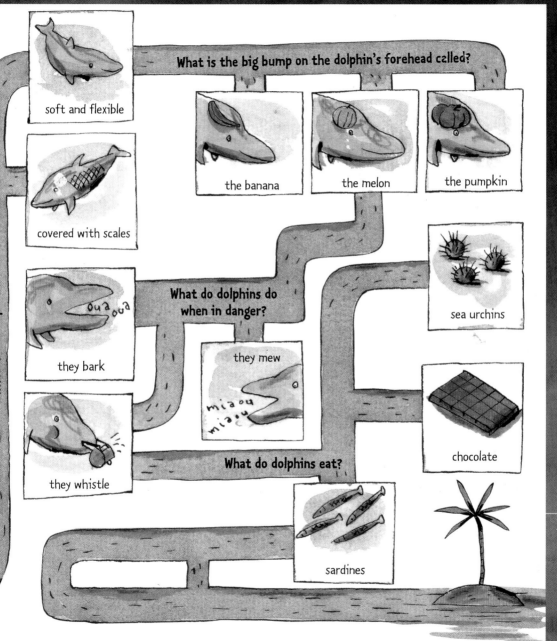

What is the dolphin's skin like?

soft and flexible

covered with scales

What is the big bump on the dolphin's forehead called?

the banana

the melon

the pumpkin

sea urchins

they bark

What do dolphins do when in danger?

they mew

chocolate

they whistle

What do dolphins eat?

sardines

Relatives

Dolphins belong to the same order as the whales. Some of them are solitary. Others are playful creatures that pet each other by rubbing their muzzles.

The orca is also known as the killer whale. With its knife-like teeth, it sometimes eats an entire seal or dolphin. It even dares to attack sharks.

The pilot whale is a deep diver. It goes for more than an hour and a half underwater without breathing while it catches squid.

The narwhal is also called the "unicorn of the sea." It lives in cold waters near the North Pole. The male has a long, sword-like tooth, which it uses to break holes in the ice so it can breathe.

The beluga got its name of "sea canary" because it sings all the time. It lives in frigid waters. Its white color, like snow, helps it hide against ice floes.

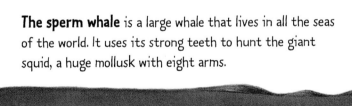

The sperm whale is a large whale that lives in all the seas of the world. It uses its strong teeth to hunt the giant squid, a huge mollusk with eight arms.

29